Jesus Tells a Story

A Linked Story Collection

Amy Willoughby-Burle

Adamant Amen Press

This is but one story of many. You are part of His story too.

CONTENTS

1. Jesus Hangs Out With Arthur at the Hospital — 1

2. Jesus Buys a Pair of Tevas — 4

3. Jesus Gets Goosebumps — 8

4. Jesus Takes a Job at the Kimchi Taco Food Truck — 12

5. Jesus Does Community Theater in His Spare Time — 16

6. Jesus Enjoys a Food Fight in the Hospital Cafeteria — 19

7. Jesus Takes a Comedy Class — 23

8. Jesus Helps Plan the Wedding — 27

9. Jesus Goes on Social Media — 31

10. Jesus Delivers for FedEx — 34

11. Jesus Goes to the County Fair — 38

12. Jesus Drives a '65 Mustang — 42

13. Jesus Ignores Visiting Hours — 46

Acknowledgements — 50

About the Author — 51

Help Us Share His Story — 52

1

Jesus Hangs Out With Arthur at the Hospital

Jesus could just as easily be in the cafeteria as He was anywhere at all, Arthur figures. So even though Arthur planned to go to the chapel, he stops at the cafeteria instead.

And Jesus is there, of course.

Jesus gets a lot of double takes from people on their way in and out of the cafeteria. Most of the time folks chuckle to themselves and keep going. No one stops to ask if it's really Him like they would if they thought He were Henry Cavill. But then you'd be talking about Superman, and Jesus doesn't want to ponder whether people think that He or Superman would come out ahead in a battle for supreme power. He knows the answer to that, but He knows some people don't agree with Him these days.

Arthur has Jesus on his mind when he gets to the cafeteria and takes a seat. He imagines Jesus, man of the people, eating at one of the wobbly, metal tables night after night. Folks praying so hard He can't get a moment to eat His banana pudding.

Arthur is pulled from his thoughts when his adult daughter, Sharon, places two trays on the table and sits down across from him. For long moments they say nothing.

"Dad," Sharon finally says softly, the tears Arthur has dreaded finally coming into his daughter's eyes. She puts her hand on his. "We need to say goodbye to Andy."

Arthur shakes his head and slides his hand out from under hers. Arthur is already sick of the fluorescent lights of the cafeteria and wants to step outside into the darkness of one last simple evening. But that evening is already gone, passed without him noticing it. By this evening, everything will be different and Arthur doesn't think he can survive it.

He can't talk about Andy so he talks about Jesus. "Do you think Jesus likes banana pudding?"

"Dad," Sharon says but decides to let him talk about whatever he wants to talk about.

"Do you think He's gotten tired of doing miracles?" Arthur asks. "Maybe they've lost their luster. Cure a leper—pretty impressive. Heal the blind—not a bad trick. But nowadays a good doctor and a bottle of pills can pretty much do that."

If only. Arthur rethinks his position. There's no way out of this that leaves Andy alive and Arthur doesn't know how he's going to talk about his son in the past tense. How do fathers talk about their sons like that? He was supposed to tell people about Andy's new job, his fiancée, their upcoming wedding, the baby they'd have one day, the two-story house in the suburbs they'd move to once Andy got his dream job. That's what the other men on the golf course talk about.

Arthur felt bad for Erin; she was a nice girl who didn't plan to end up widowed before she ever got married. Andy had almost rallied and they thought he might recover, but then he suffered a blood pressure crash and then a spike that put him into a semi-coma and pretty much fried his brain. No one wants to hear about that on the 9th hole. No one wants to watch a grown man cry.

Andy doesn't mean to make his father sad, but it's just the way this one is meant to go. If Arthur could turn the daytime sky black and send a noise so loud it shook the earth, he'd do it, just like God did. All fathers would, the ones who watch their sons stop breathing.

Arthur already hates that people will temper his grief for him by pointing out that his son had been sick for so long and *really, isn't it better now that he's out of pain?* He'll probably even say that too, which really ticks him off because all he really wants to do is cry and punch someone in the face.

Andy has been in and out of the hospital over the years and most of the time they jokingly referred to it as routine maintenance, to be expected with cases like his. They've done the Holiday in the Hospital too many times to count. Andy has Summered on the 7th Floor. They referred to the hospital as their second home in the city. Andy has beaten the odds before, but there's no coming back this time.

Arthur looks at the clock on the cafeteria wall just over Sharon's shoulder and then closes his eyes. Not much time left. *"It shouldn't take long,"* the nurse had said about the process of letting Andy die. The nurse was young and her haircut told Arthur she didn't have kids. No one with kids has time for hair like that.

Jesus knew that Arthur was wrong about the girl. In her own way, she had meant it as a comfort. He didn't expect her to realize that it wasn't just the moment between breathing and death that she was talking about. Losing his son would take the rest of Arthur's life.

2

Jesus Buys a Pair of Tevas

Eventually, He'd have to replace those old sandals. He's not trying to be stylish; it's just a necessity. After 2000 years, a man could use a new pair of shoes.

Inside the shoe store the air smells of leather and plastic and sweat. Jesus wanders the aisles until a young girl approaches and introduces herself. She doesn't need to. It's Erin; she's engaged to Andy. Andy is dying in the hospital. Jesus knows her. He knows everything about it.

Erin looks at Jesus's feet. "You're rocking the Jesus sandals," she says.

"Thank you," He replies. The low timbre of His voice out loud inside the small store causes the other patrons to look toward the warm sound.

"You'll like these," Erin says and pulls down a pair with a camouflage pattern in greens and grays.

"Those," He says, pointing to a bright orange pair, stepping up His game a notch.

Blending in wasn't what He came here to do, but He's been going around unseen all the same. Despite His penchant for performing miracles, flashy isn't really His thing. Then again, He didn't do them for attention, even though He got it. He did want people to hear what

He had to say. It was important and still is. And He loves people. He likes making things better. He knows people don't think so because He hears them ask why He doesn't do it all the time. It's the question He's asked the most. The one that people least understand how to accept the answer to.

"I'll find your size," she says and heads for the back of the store.

Jesus slips off His old sandals and runs His hand over the scars on the tops of His feet. Erin is back quickly and kneels down in front of Him. She looks at His feet and her mouth forms a little circle of surprise.

"I could find you another brand that crosses over the top," she says, sitting back on her heels. "If you want to cover those up."

"Oh, I don't mind them," Jesus says. "It was a long time ago."

"So what did you do?" she asks.

"I let myself get nailed to a cross," Jesus says—not to shock her; it's just the answer to the question.

"Oh, my," she says. "Why would you do that?"

She looks up at Him and He smiles at her. His heart blooms in His chest. He knows people don't believe it, but He just loves them all so much.

"I'll take these," He says and slips them on His feet.

"Would you like a box for the other pair?" she asks. "Take them home with you?"

"Sure," Jesus says.

At the register, she rings up His purchase and He produces a hundred dollar bill from the hem of His sleeve. He doesn't get very much of it back, but He doesn't need it. He pushes the change across the counter to her.

"For your troubles," He says.

She shakes her head but eats up the small amount of money with her eyes. She puts her hand on the counter as if she is going to take the money, but she doesn't.

"We aren't allowed to take tips," she says, warily.

"You need gas in your car," Jesus says, which is true, but ambiguous enough.

She tilts her head and prepares to decline. She has never been one to complain, an honorable trait that He admires. She is also slow to ask for help, often to her own detriment, and He wishes she would reach out. Especially now that life is going to be different than she thought it was.

She'll find another young man in some years' time, but getting over Andy is going to be hard. She had planned to go back to school to get her nursing degree, but she's spent so much time in the hospital already she's not sure she can go back there. She's not ready to figure out what to do instead of marrying Andy. She thought they might get a cat when she moved in. Her roommate right now is allergic to cats.

She'll also need to keep this job, but she's one more call-out from being fired. There's nothing she can do about it. *It is what it is*—she's in the habit of saying. Especially now when Andy's days are short and she wants to be there for the rest of them, shoe sales don't seem that important.

"Your paycheck is short this week," Jesus says, and places His hand on top of hers. "You should be by your fiancé's side as much as you can." Time for ambiguity over.

The salesgirl looks at Jesus's hand on the top of hers and sucks in a sharp breath. Jesus knows that He hasn't frightened her though. She reaches her other hand out and touches the scars at his wrists. He is as moved as she is. It isn't often that people stop long enough to recognize Him.

"Thank you," she says, her voice quivering, and she moves her hands from his and puts the money quickly into her pocket.

"Of course," He says, "is there anything else I can do for you?"

He could slide another bill from His sleeve, but He knows what she really needs.

She puts her hand on the shoebox that now holds the old pair of sandals. "May I keep these?"

He nods. It's an unusual request—but He's really not here to judge. And besides, He knows what she means. All He has is hers; all she needs to do is ask.

3

— • —

JESUS GETS GOOSEBUMPS

Streets of this city are far more crowded than the ones in His tiny hometown of Nazareth. Everyone knew everyone there and getting lost in a crowd was something you'd have to venture over to Sepphoris to do. Jesus had gone to the city a time or two with his father, Joseph, looking for work. Jesus was a builder like His pop and the city was in need of builders after it had been destroyed. Rebuilding would become something Jesus was very good at.

Now, in this city, He's not strolling the sidewalk long before someone calls out to Him.

"Jesus, right?" asks the man stopped in front of Him.

"Yes," Jesus says and almost calls the man by name as well, but He knows the man thinks He's only a street performer in costume and He doesn't want to freak the guy out.

"I knew it," the man says, jabbing his finger toward Jesus in triumph. "So what do you do?"

Jesus chuckles and thinks about breaking into a show tune refrain—maybe "What's the Buzz." He likes that one. He can almost see the whole production right here on the street corner. He could round up some of the other performers and they would probably do a solid job on the fly. He's not trying to be a superstar, but the songs are catchy. Maybe He'll see about doing some community theater one day.

"I save people," Jesus answers the man. "You know, show them the way to heaven."

And all that jazz.

"Right on, dude," the man says, giving Jesus the "thumbs up" and nodding, "Keeping it real."

Indeed.

The man looks around, takes off his own ball cap and puts it at Jesus's feet.

"You need a way to collect tips, dude," the man says. "Don't stand out here and do your thing for nothing."

The man tosses a dollar into his donated hat. "For the work of the church," he says and winks at Jesus. "See you around, dude."

"Yes, I hope so," Jesus says and He means that.

He picks up the hat, takes out the dollar and wiggles the cap onto His head. He toggles the brim back and forth to settle the hat better over His hair. He chuckles at himself; more comfortable than the last thing He wore on His head, but He isn't sure He's a ball cap kind of guy. He pockets the hat for later and hands the dollar to the first homeless person He sees.

"God bless you," the man says sincerely.

Jesus studies His reflection in the shoe store window where he just bought a new pair of Tevas. Yes, He looks better without the hat. No sense in making it even harder for people to see Him. The salesgirl in the store is setting a display in the shop window. He catches her eye and waves. She smiles at Him and waves back. He points to His shoes and gives a thumbs up. Her smile widens.

A little farther down the crowded street He's recognized again. A young boy, only five years old, looks up at Jesus and yanks on his grandfather's sleeve to get his attention. Jesus waves to the boy and smiles.

Jesus had known even as a child that His life would speed toward its purpose soon enough. He knows that of this boy, too. Important things are ahead and Jesus gets a flutter in His Heart just thinking about what this little boy will grow up to do. It isn't time for the little lad to know yet, but one day he will change things for the better. Many years from now. Many childhood afternoons, many classes in college, a wife, kids, and a growing realization about the world that he won't be able to turn his head from. Jesus is proud of him already. It will be a hard battle and he'll fight it well.

Jesus winks at him and the little boy winks back.

When his grandfather registers the tugging but doesn't entertain the boy's insistence to *Look, Grandpop. Look who it is* Jesus intervenes. "Hey there, Bob."

The boy's grandpop looks up then. He obviously expects to see a neighbor or an old co-worker but when his eyes light on Jesus's, Bob startles.

The little boy asks, "Do you know Him, Grandpop?"

"Maybe," Bob says, looking at Jesus the way you do when you think you remember someone from long ago but can't quite place who it is.

Jesus claps Bob on the shoulder and then bends down to the little boy. "Take good care of your grandpop. I'll see you again soon."

Kneeling on one knee, Jesus holds still while the little boy touches His beard, His scars, His clothes. The boy scans Jesus's face and looks deeply into His eyes.

"See you soon," the boy says, standing up straight. Already he knows something is different. He doesn't know what just yet, but that day will come.

Jesus stands up and touches Bob's shoulder. He'll see Bob again, too.

Jesus watches the little boy disappear into the crowd of lives he will one day change. That will be a story for another time. Jesus feels the little hairs on His arms stand up. Yep, even Jesus can get goosebumps.

4

— · —

JESUS TAKES A JOB AT THE KIMCHI TACO FOOD TRUCK

Ultimately, Jesus doesn't need the money; that's not what it's about. He's interested in the idea of a kimchi taco. It uses some sort of flatbread and the insides are different, but the end result is similar. He also likes the idea of having a job. A sense of purpose in this place where people have forgotten Him. And the truck is cool. It's orange and teal and Jesus likes the easy pass-through window where people tell Him what they want and He gives it to them. He knows it can't always work that way, but He wishes it could.

He misses having coworkers too—a band of buds working side by side for a common goal. He thinks the apostles would have liked the idea of a food truck. They could have driven around Galilee and Judea feeding the hungry. They would have named the truck *Loaves and Fishes*. Sure, a food truck is far less miraculous than the way He did it the first time, but it would have been fun. Of course Peter would have wanted to drive. Jesus would ride shotgun and they'd get one of those bumper stickers that said "God is my Co-Pilot."

"Thanks for taking the position, chief," the Korean gentleman who runs the truck says. "You wouldn't believe how hard it is to get someone to work for nothing. Everybody wants the world to be a better place, but no one has time to make that happen."

The truck, called *Hey Man, It's Kimchi Taco*, serves leftovers from the Korean buffet, giving away free "tacos" to the poor and homeless, so it's a natural fit for Jesus. He's a sucker for the underdog.

"We need more bleeding hearts like you, chief," Eun-woo says and hands Jesus a hair net. "I'll look for something for the beard," he says and points at Jesus's face. "Even poor people want food without hair in it, you know. They still deserve the best."

"Yes," Jesus says, his soft voice filling the inside of the truck with warmth, "they do."

A young woman wearing hospital scrubs and toting a small child on her hip orders two tacos. Alison. He knows her well. She's one of Andy's nurses. Her son's father is in jail for making bad decisions. Jesus still loves him though, of course. Still, he knows that Alison needs someone who can love her and her son the way they need. Jesus will help her find him. And He'll look after the boy's father as well.

"Two tacos," Jesus says and hands her a tray.

She looks at the tray and then back at Jesus. "There are four here," she says and tries to hand the tray back to him.

"There's plenty to go around," Jesus replies, refusing to take the tray back. They're supposed to give one taco per person to make sure they don't run out. Jesus isn't worried about that. He smiles at the small child. Jesus holds up a finger, telling Alison to wait. He turns to the refrigerator and retrieves a cup of strawberry yogurt and a container of fruit.

"He'll like this better, yes?" Jesus asks, already knowing the answer. "You can save the tacos you don't finish for later."

"Thank you," Alison says, letting the little boy slip off her hip to stand beside her as Jesus slides the tacos over on the tray so that He can place the child's food there as well. "These are his favorites," she says, ashamed of the help she needs. She touches her hair almost apologetically. She spent too much money on a new haircut. She knows she shouldn't have but she just wanted one nice thing.

Jesus touches His hand to hers. He searches her face until her eyes meet His. He nods at her. "Enjoy your meal." He reaches back into the fridge and pulls out two cans of ginger ale.

"How do you have all these things?" she asks and shakes her head. "We come here every Tuesday, and the other guy never has anything but kimchi."

Jesus winks at her and tells her again to enjoy her meal and to come back anytime.

Jesus goes back to work making more tacos.

"I wish we had some meat today," Eun-woo laments. "I only ever have kimchi. I'd like to give them more."

"I think I saw some meat in the fridge," Jesus replies and the man turns to look for it.

"I don't see it, chief."

"Keep looking," Jesus says. "Seek and ye shall find." Jesus chuckles to Himself.

"Oh look, beef bulgogi," the man says and brings a tray over to the prep counter. "So, where are you from, chief? You got a bit of an accent. It's nice not to be the only funny sounding one around here." He makes air quotes around "funny sounding." People give him a hard time too often for things that are really just normal.

"Nazareth." Jesus offers the easier answer. Heaven throws people for a loop.

"Like Jesus?" the man asks. "You been over here long?"

"A while," Jesus says.

"You ever go back?" Eun-woo asks.

"I did once," Jesus says, remembering. "Dragged out of town by the sleeve of my robe."

"What did you do?" the man asks and elbows Jesus playfully. "Make some gal's husband angry?"

"I made everyone angry," Jesus says.

"Well," Eun-woo says, "I'm sure things went better for you after that."

Jesus chuckles again. "Things are good today," He says, a fan of living in the moment. "Worry not," He likes to say. "Let's serve some of that bulgogi."

He likes the sound of the word. *Bulgogi.* It feels like bubbles in His mouth.

"Thanks for the help, chief," Eun-woo says. "God looks on you with favor."

Jesus looks at the man and smiles at him. "You as well."

It feels nice to be of service. He doesn't need the thanks, but He appreciates it.

"Will you come back tomorrow?" the man asks.

"Of course," Jesus says. "Let's serve japchae tomorrow. It will be a nice change."

"If we have any," says Eun-woo doubtfully.

"We will," Jesus says.

Yes, Peter would have liked the idea of a food truck. They would have had a good run of it—driving the dusty streets, passing out food and turning water to wine. Peter was great with a crowd—a little brash sometimes, but he had a nice smile. Jesus likes to see people smile.

5

Jesus Does Community Theater in His Spare Time

Shoo-in, He thought—*Jesus Christ Superstar* and all, but the director says He's trying too hard.

"You're a bit too ..." the man says, waving his hand through the air between them.

"Too authentic?" Jesus offers.

"No," the director says flippantly. "You just don't have leading man looks."

He's right. Jesus isn't a Ted Neely or Jim Caviezel or Christian Bale or one of the other men who have played Him on stage or screen, men to whom His father gave more than their fair share of good looks. He's just an average Joshua as far as attractiveness goes. That was part of the plan.

"I'll put you down for Judas," the director says, snapping his fingers. "He's central to the plot, you know."

"I do," Jesus says and shakes his head. *Poor Judas.*

"Have you seen the play?" the director asks.

Jesus shrugs. "I know how the story goes," He says.

"I'm thinking about doing something radical with this production," the director says with the sort of confidence people have when they don't know what they're talking about. "An alternate ending perhaps. Imagine this." He claps Jesus on the shoulder and then waves his hand out in front of them both the way people do when they do indeed want you to imagine something. He says, "Judas comes to his senses. Jesus doesn't die. It's a happy ending."

"Is it?" Jesus asks.

The director seems quite taken with his plot twist. "I can see it now. Jesus gets married, has some kids; maybe He does some party tricks now and then just to keep His superpowers fresh. You know, turns some water into wine at the Christmas party."

"Do you think there would still be Christmas?" Jesus asks.

"Sure," the director says. "Everyone likes to put up a tree."

"The lights are pretty," Jesus agrees.

The director grabs a copy of the script and starts paging through it. He loses sight of Jesus standing there beside him and starts talking to himself about revisions. "Judas still has to turn Jesus in. Jesus has to get to Pilate, or else we lose a good chunk of the play."

"Some of the most important parts," Jesus says, but the director isn't listening.

"Judas could team up with Pilate," the director says, making a thoughtful face. "Like a buddy cop thing. They could sneak Jesus out of the temple. Maybe put him in a witness protection program just before the guards came to take him away."

Jesus nods and offers, "Then no one would know who He was and He could go through the rest of time unnoticed."

The director points at Him. "Brilliant."

Jesus sighs. But He isn't upset at the guy. The man just wants to be remembered. Wants to leave his mark. And Jesus certainly knows how it feels to do something radical.

"We're going to have to rework the songs, though," the director says, suddenly a little less excited. "And then there's all the fake blood we bought for the scourging."

Jesus winces. He could have done without that part. Then again, He really could have done without the whole thing. It wasn't His best day.

But of course, it wasn't His day. It was everyone else's day.

He remembers talking to His father in the garden, though. Asking for a rewrite. A plot twist. A different ending. He had liked the job He had before His ministry began. He was good at building things. He might have gotten married if He didn't have to spend all His time doing miracles and teaching the masses. What if Pilate had set Him free? What if Judas hadn't turned Him in? What if He'd come out of the garden with a new plot after all? What if He had chosen not to do any of it?

No, He couldn't imagine such things. It all went just the way it was supposed to go. He's happy with the plot of His story.

The director rushes back over to Him. "Change of plans, dude," he says to Jesus. "If you still want the part, it's yours. Fred flaked out and now we've got no lead. You think you can handle the role?"

Oh yes. He can. Radical had been worth every moment. Even without the catchy songs.

Jesus's eyes shine with conviction and without hesitation He says, "I was born for it."

6

— · —

Jesus Enjoys a Food Fight in the Hospital Cafeteria

Leaving Andy's room while the nurses do what they do, Sharon had found her father in the hospital cafeteria, which was not where she expected to. It's a miracle she found the place at all, what with the maze of corridors and elevators that only go to certain floors. As if spending days in the hospital isn't disorienting enough. A young nurse had told her to follow the yellow lines on the floor. Sharon had laughed unexpectedly and asked the girl if it led to the wizard or the wicked witch. The nurse had looked confused and a little sad. Sharon clicked her heels but she didn't go back home to the way things were before this terrible dream began.

"Are you ok?" the nurse had asked.

"The yellow lines, then," Sharon had said in exasperated confirmation.

Luckily, she did find the cafeteria.

Jesus found it too and now He sits at a table by the door while Sharon talks to her dad. Jesus really wants to speak with her, but she's engaged for the moment holding up her end of the ridiculous conversation Arthur has started. Her father has always been a religious man, but lately and understandably, he's been talking about Jesus more than usual. Today it's about what sort of car Jesus might drive.

"The car's a classic," Arthur is saying and Sharon knows he's just trying not to think about Andy up in the ICU where nothing can help him anymore.

"You don't think he'd want something newer?" Sharon asks now about the car, stabbing a pea from the terrible plate of food she got for each of them but depositing the green orb back on her plate without eating it. "Something to show He's up with the times."

"That's just the thing," Arthur says. "Jesus doesn't need a Lincoln Navigator with Bluetooth capabilities and a GPS."

Sharon drives a Lincoln Navigator with Bluetooth capabilities and a GPS. She sees her father wince and knows he feels bad. She tries not to read into the comment and get upset about the possible commentary on her spending habits that her father might or might not be making. She decides to let the car comment slide. Impending grief has been good therapy for them in the past. When her mother died, she and her dad and Andy had clung to all the good parts of their relationships for quite a while. Sharon likes feeling closer to her father now, but the trade-off will most likely be the death of her. What will she do without her little brother? He's been here with her for thirty-three years. It hasn't been long enough.

"I don't know," Sharon says, and sighs. "There are a few more streets out here than there were back in the day. Stop lights and Starbucks and even the Lord could get distracted and miss His turn-off."

Sharon figures no one would blame Jesus if He spent too much money on a vintage convertible and hit the road. Sharon reaches across the table, putting her hand over Arthur's again.

Jesus knows that Arthur is so desperate for her touch that it burns just a little. He wishes Sharon knew that too and would hold on just a little tighter sometimes.

"I think you're right, Dad," Sharon says, an olive branch. "Jesus surely doesn't need a car with GPS."

"That voice makes me crazy," Arthur says and then affects the cadence of the GPS voice. "Jesus already knows to *'turn right at the next light.'* He doesn't need to be told he has *'arrived at his destination,'*"

Sharon smiles. The first in a while. Her father is funny. He'd actually been doing a comedy class recently—before this last bad turn. Andy was going to sign up for the class too. He has the same sense of humor. Had the same sense? No, not past tense just yet.

"Besides," Arthur says. "Jesus is retro. He's old school."

"You don't think Jesus would want power locks and windows though?" Sharon asks, pushing another pea across the plate with her fork. Andy always hated peas. She sees him suddenly in her mind, decades ago, in his highchair tossing peas on the floor when their mother wasn't looking. Sharon wonders if Andy will see their mother in Heaven. She wonders if there really is a Heaven.

Arthur holds his hands up and out in front of him catching her attention again. "Behold I say, unlock. And it is unlocked," Arthur says.

Sharon laughs but then the swell of emotion turns to tears.

"Sweetheart," Arthur says softly. "We'll make it through this. You and me."

That makes her cry harder. She knows her father wants to cry too. He's just being strong for her sake. She wipes her hand across her face to dry the tears and something small hits her cheek. She looks up to see that Arthur is holding a spoonful of peas like a catapult. Tears flow down her cheeks again but she's smiling. He remembers Andy and his dislike of peas too. He remembers everything, just like she does.

She loads her spoon as well.

"Three, two, one," Sharon counts down and peas fly through the air across the table. Little green over-cooked pellets smack into their laughing faces and splat onto the floor.

"Again," Arthur shouts, and heads turn to find the source of the strangely jubilant emotion. "For Andy!"

Arthur and Sharon load up, fire the peas, and laugh through their flowing tears.

A pea lands in Jesus's banana pudding. He chuckles. Maybe He'll take a comedy class too. Laughing feels nice.

Sharon and Arthur see security coming and flee from the cafeteria, following the yellow lines back to Andy. Jesus is already there waiting for them.

7

— · —

JESUS TAKES A COMEDY CLASS

Overall, Jesus is happy with the way the gospels were written—all the pertinent info was recorded and He liked the way that among the four of them, the guys got it all sorted out. But even though there's no record of it, Jesus liked to laugh too. The story didn't warrant a quirky sidekick, but some comic relief wouldn't have been the worst thing. He could see how the natural instinct was to keep things serious. It was pretty serious. He died for it after all. So did a lot of people.

Still, He wants people to know that He understands the whole "human" thing. If He had the notion, He might put out a director's cut of The Bible. For instance, He had cried more than just that one time. And He'd worried more than that night in the garden. He was human after all and it was a hard thing to be.

So, He's grateful for laughter. He loves the way it tickles first at the corners of His mouth. And the way it bubbles up His face creating a slight watering of the eyes and that's just the smile preceding it. The actual laugh itself is heavenly. The way the lips part and the mouth opens to let out the very sound of angels. At its strongest, the laugh wells up in the chest, rumbles up the throat, and shakes the whole body with bliss.

He needs to laugh again. So Jesus decides to take a comedy class. There's a spot open since Andy didn't show up. Jesus will tell him all about it the next time He and Andy talk.

"Biblical comedy," the teacher says, gesturing at Jesus's clothes. "What's your name?"

"Jesus."

The man chuckles. Jesus is pleased; already He's on a roll.

"Where you from, Jesus?" the teacher asks, nodding, setting up the next part of the joke.

"Nazareth."

"I love that you're all in, dude," the teacher says, pointing at Jesus emphatically. "Committed to the part."

"I am."

The students all take turns on the mic to reveal their schtick. But everyone is so angry. This isn't comedy. It's pain. Well, Jesus thinks, He's a natural at dealing with people's pain, too. Perhaps this is exactly where He needs to be.

When His turn on the mic comes, He does a few of Peter's old jokes—crickets. They were funnier back in the day.

Jeffrey, the saddest chap in class, claps Jesus on the shoulder when He sits back down. "Guess you had to be there, huh, man?" Jeffrey says.

"I'm doing the best I can," Jesus says.

He knows Jeffrey is too. He's doing better than most people in his shape would be. Beaten down from the inside. Struggling just to stand up each day and try again. Jeffrey has forgotten how special he is. He used to know and his light radiated out from him so strong the people around him couldn't stand to look at it. They beat him down because of it. People are jealous and bitter sometimes. More pain. Jesus is determined to turn that light back on inside Jeffrey.

Jeffrey takes his turn at the mic and bombs.

"I shouldn't let it bother me," Jeffrey says, slumping in the chair. "I should be more like you. You're not afraid to get up there and say something that people boo at. What's the worst that could happen, right?"

Jesus laughs. Right out loud. The laughter pours out of him sudden and fantastic. The sound of it carries across the room on angel wings. A large, white feather drifts down from the ceiling and lands on Jeffrey's foot.

Jesus smiles.

It's starting.

"How'd you do that?" Jeffrey asks, looking up. "Was that magic?"

Jeffrey reaches down and picks up the feather. He can feel it trill between his fingers. His eyes dart to Jesus in shock and wonder and sheer hope. Jeffrey hears a faint sound and holds the feather to his ear and listens. The soft sound of laughter tickles against his cheek. Jesus reaches over and plucks another feather from Jeffrey's hair.

"What is this?" Jeffrey asks.

"It's the happiness you're looking for," Jesus says.

Jeffrey's eyes pool with tears. But they aren't the sad tears he usually cries as soon as his head hits the pillow and memories drown him again and again. Jesus recognizes these tears and the feeling in the back of the throat that comes with them. These are hopeful tears. Maybe-I'll-give-it-one-more-shot tears.

Jeffrey holds out his hands like a child and feathers float down from the ceiling, flickering in the stage lights, falling across his upturned face. Jeffrey clutches the white feathers in his fingers and folds them to his chest. More and more and more falling, unstoppable, floating around the room, drifting down to cover his boots.

"Where is this coming from?" Jeffrey says, looking up toward the ceiling like there's a bag of feathers being dumped down on him like in a play.

"They're coming from me," Jesus says, a lump forming hard in His throat. The happy ball of emotion forms each time one of His children realizes how much He loves them, how deeply He wants them, and how completely special He knows each of them to be.

Jeffrey looks at Jesus and sees Him. Jeffrey smiles, his eyes wet with happy tears. "Do we have to clean this up before we go?"

Jeffrey is just the best. "They'll come with us," Jesus says and motions Jeffrey to follow him. The feathers stir around and float with them right out the door and into the world where everything has changed.

"It's bright out here," Jeffrey says. "Do other people see the feathers?"

"I hope so," Jesus says. He puts his arm around Jeffrey's shoulder.

"Me too," Jeffrey says and puts his arm around Jesus in return.

There's that lump in Jesus's throat again. Man, He loves this part.

This is going in the director's cut. The one written in Jesus's heart. He and Jeffrey are going to spend a lot more time laughing.

"Do you like kimchi tacos?" Jesus asks. "Want to meet me for lunch tomorrow? I want to introduce you to someone."

"By the hospital?" Jeffrey asks. "I've been meaning to try that food truck."

"I think you'll be happy with what you find," Jesus says.

"I have this crazy feeling it might be the best meal of my life," Jeffrey says and the feathers swirling alongside them rise up and flutter all around.

Jesus laughs. Man, He loves it when things come together like this. Yep, the director's cut indeed.

8

JESUS HELPS PLAN THE WEDDING

Venturing across town, Jesus stops in to help Maggie with the wedding plans. Her son, Sam, is getting married and she's thrilled for him, really. But Sam is only six months out of rehab and every big, new thing scares Maggie. It took him six hard years to get to rehab and every one of those days feels like it was yesterday. She remembers when he was six and told her everything, everything, everything. By the time he was sixteen all she got was half-lies and talking to him was like pulling out that prickly weed from the garden that you don't remember will sting you until your whole hand is wrapped around it. Then one day he was twenty-six and had been lost in the dark forest of depression for so long they almost didn't recognize him when he turned up on the doorstep drunk, disoriented, and disheartened.

Maggie tries to keep her focus on the wedding planning, but her mind is prone to wander. Often, like today, she ends up just sitting at her kitchen table looking out the window making lists of things she can see. The grass is green and it needs to be mowed. There are three birds on the feeder—all of them a different size and color. In the sky there is a cloud shaped like a dinosaur and next to it, one shaped like a slice of pizza the size of the dinosaur's head. She wonders how much pizza a dinosaur could eat. She's easily distracted, so Jesus has taken over most of the details.

When He knocked on the door the first day, because just appearing at Maggie's kitchen table would have been startling to say the least—Maggie thought He was a friend of her soon-to-be daughter-in-law's who had come over to help out. He is a friend, so He didn't correct her.

"Rachel is kind to include me in the planning," Maggie tells Jesus as they sit together at the table. "Sam is lucky to have her. Rachel really is a saint," Maggie says.

"There are everyday saints all around us," Jesus says.

Maggie nods, thinking this hippie friend of Rachel's is quite profound.

"Sam has put her through so much," Maggie says, grateful that Rachel sticks by him. "Do you know Sam, too?"

"I do," Jesus says, His voice bright.

"Sam's best friend, Andy, is dying," Maggie says matter of factly. "Did you know that?"

Andy is supposed to be the best man in the wedding, but he's taken a sharp turn toward the end and even though Sam says he's ok about it all, Maggie worries.

Jesus reaches across the table, past the wedding planning bits and pieces and puts His hand over Maggie's.

"What's next on the list?" Jesus asks. The task at hand helps Maggie to stay busy.

So far Jesus and Maggie have picked out flowers and done a cake tasting. All the cake seemed to taste the same to Maggie so Jesus picked the lemon and honey cake with buttercream frosting with just a hint of lavender. Not so much lavender that it tastes like soap, but just that amount that makes it taste lovely and you're not sure why. You find yourself going back for another slice and another and you finally ask, "What is in this icing?" and someone says, "Lavender." "Ah," you say. "Of course. I should have known" and you get one more slice.

Now, they're almost done with the planning. Jesus looks at the poster board seating chart they're workingork on. Each person's name is flagged to a button so you can move them around like in a game. Maggie's got it pretty organized, but Jesus knows that Aunt Betty and her sister Patricia just got into a banger of an argument, *again,* and it's going to last awhile, *again.* Jesus picks up the buttons and holds them in his hands. Maggie doesn't know about this fight yet, but she nods agreement, impressed that Rachel's friend would guess at the likely animosity.

"Sit Patricia with the Montana cousins," Maggie says. "They don't know how ornery she is."

Jesus places Patricia's button at table four and sighs. She can hold a grudge with the best of them, but it's not anger that rules her. It's sadness. It's the way Patricia feels about herself. Worthless. Which breaks Jesus's heart. He suffered that day for her too. She's worth everything to Him.

Maggie picks up the button with Sam's name on it. Maggie knows that Sam wishes she wouldn't worry about him all the time. Jesus wishes Maggie didn't worry so much too, but He knows that's just what mothers do. He thinks about His own mother and everything He put her through. Running away to the temple was small potatoes compared to that last day.

Jesus knows that Sam will be alright, but there are still hard days to come. Even when Maggie hears the soft voice in her heart telling her things will be ok, Jesus understands that it's hard to watch it happen knowing there's nothing she can do but be there.

Jesus remembers seeing His mother looking up at Him from the bottom of the cross. Her eyes filled with love and pain, but she was with Him when He needed her. And when else had He needed His mama more? Being there matters.

Sam is grown now and Maggie knows her role has changed. It's not her job to ask if he's taking his medication. It's not her job to ask if he's seeing his therapist. It's not her job to ask if he's ok.

It's her job to remind him of the little boy who hunted for treasure along the trails handing her a rock, a robin feather, a piece of dried moss. It's her job to help him take care of his heart. To help him remember to hope.

And it's Jesus's job to do the same for her. He loves His job. Jesus places His hand on Maggie's shoulder. She feels better already.

9

JESUS GOES ON SOCIAL MEDIA

Evidently, He needs to do some rebranding. At best He's getting a bad rap with the public. At worst, they're forgetting Him altogether. He's been watching a series of videos on YouTube about marketing and building your platform. The presenter insists that you need a social media presence. Apparently He needs to get some friends and build a following. It's a daunting task to start from scratch, but He's done it before. So He sets up an Instagram account because He likes the pretty pictures even though He knows the mess that lies just outside the frame.

He sees that He needs a catchy handle. @therealjc, taken. @Jesusofnazarethofficial, taken—really? There's even a picture, crown of thorns and all. Maybe He'll skip Instagram for now. So He gets a Facebook account instead. The lady on YouTube says that you should pick three words that describe what you stand for and put those in your bio. His are pretty easy: love, forgiveness, grace. But people seem to have gotten confused: judgement, self-righteousness, hate. That's not right at all.

The lady on YouTube says to make sure you put a picture of yourself on your account. You are your brand, she says. He takes a selfie with His cell phone, which no one calls Him on but that's ok.

He feels a little unsure about using His actual face on his profile, but everyone's always wondering what He really looks like, so He loads it up. It's weird to see Himself in the little circle by His name. Yeshua.

"Be authentic," the YouTube lady says.

Facebook suggests some folks that He might know, and He does, of course. He already knows everybody, but He wants them to know Him too. The lady on YouTube says that if you send out friend requests, other people will start to friend you too. He likes the use of the word *friend* as a verb. After a day or two of scrolling, He comes across Patricia. Her profile picture is a cartoon cat. She has thirty-two friends. A fair amount of them are fake accounts. She doesn't know this. She's lucky if a post gets two likes and most get no comments at all. But Patricia posts every day, five or six times on some days. Every day the posts start out cheerful—comments about the flowers in her window pot, her cat lying in the sun. She's trying. But as the day winds down, so does Patricia. Her posts get melancholy, their accompanying pictures darker and more despairing. She's a good photographer, Jesus notes, but He's sad that she is sad. Jesus knows that she just wants to feel like someone hears her, sees her, gives a hoot about anything she says.

Jesus does see her and hear her and yes, Jesus gives a hoot. He starts to comment on her posts. At first she doesn't even notice it. She's so used to no one replying that she doesn't even bother to look. So He tags her. Yeshua is with Patricia and he posts a picture of the bench she likes to sit on along the edge of the pond at the park not far from her house. #comesitwithme, He writes. #Imtherewaiting.

Patricia sees it. She comes to the bench where He's been sitting all morning enjoying the way the sunlight dances across the water. That's one of His favorite things. Maybe He'll take a pic and post it. But that can wait. He's going to hang with Patricia for a while.

He stands when He feels her approach. He holds out His hand to her. Patricia gasps just a little. She didn't think it would really be Him, but she was willing to take a shot.

"It's you," she says.

"In the flesh," He says and smiles at her.

She chuckles, getting His sense of humor. "You're funny," she says, surprised but pleased.

"I appreciate that," He says and gestures to the bench.

They sit together looking out at the water. Patricia glances at Him when she thinks He's not looking. He looks exactly like she thought he would.

After an hour of just sitting there with her, she figures He's got places to be.

"You don't have to stay here," she says. "I know you're busy."

"I'm all yours," He says. "What do you want to talk about?"

"What do you want to hear?"

"All of it," He says. "Start from the top."

He shifts on the bench so that He can look fully into her face and she into his. He can't wait to hear more about her cat and her plants and when she's ready to talk about everything else, He's more than ready to listen.

10

Jesus Delivers for FedEx

Sharon keeps sending packages to Andy's house. She doesn't know what to talk to Andy about in the hospital since he's not conscious, so she shops for him online while she's visiting.

At first, when they all thought he'd be in for just a bit and then head home like usual, she'd bought the things that she figured he'd need once he got back home.

Toilet paper, trashbags, batteries, shampoo. But once it became obvious that Andy wasn't going home this time, Sharon lost herself in online shopping. She knows it's ridiculous. Andy is never going to get these items. But in the moment, she can hope.

She knows he likes comic books even though he isn't a kid anymore. He's in his early thirties but that doesn't stop him from getting excited about finding a vintage *Batman* or *Dark Knight* or whatever it is that he likes. She wishes she'd listened more closely now. So she shops on eBay for comics.

"Look at this Dee," she says, using his nickname from when they were little. "A mint condition *Legends of the Dark Knight*. Do you have that one?"

He doesn't answer.

"Let's get it," Sharon says. "Just in case."

And that's just the start. She orders him a new coffee machine, a weighted blanket, a set of Christmas throw pillows because he never thinks to decorate and she thinks that he should this year, a cat tree because he should get a cat when he gets home—his fiancée, Erin, likes cats, right? They had talked about her moving in but she hasn't yet. Maybe she will if they get a cat.

Every day packages show up on Andy's porch and then sit there until Sharon can tear herself from Andy's hospital room long enough to put the boxes, unopened, into the house. The stack of boxes gets pretty big.

It doesn't take too long before the house gets a reputation. Delivery drivers swear it's haunted or inhabited by an agoraphobic. There's debate about the one, and only one, light that is on no matter what time of day it is and speculation about the ancient jeep Cherokee with grass grown up to the tops of the tires. Everyone agrees that whatever is going on, it isn't good.

So when no one wants to deliver packages and the ones that are delivered start to get stolen, Jesus steps in. He delivers the boxes and makes sure they get placed as neatly and as inconspicuously as possible. He knows Andy doesn't need a set of vintage board games or a stand mixer in case he and Erin want to start baking, but Sharon needs him to get these things.

Jesus wants Sharon to stop buying so much. It's just putting a hole in her bank account, but what is money at a time like this?

It isn't a surprise to Jesus when He stops by the house with a shipment of ramen noodles to see that Sharon has installed a camera by the door. He heard her talking to Andy about that.

"That way we can make sure the packages are getting there and no one is taking them off the porch," she'd said to Andy who was unresponsive.

She can also tell Andy when things have arrived and then they can talk about where he'll place the new plant stand and what plants he can get when he gets home. The oxygen will do him good. Everyone loves plants.

So when Jesus sets the boxes down and waves at the camera, He knows Sharon is watching.

"Look, Dee," she says, turning the camera toward Andy's closed eyes. "The delivery guy is there."

She turns the phone back toward herself, looking at the delivery man on the screen. He's moving the boxes around so that the ones from yesterday and the new ones are stacked nicely and pushed up close to the house. It's supposed to rain later. She needs to get over there and put the boxes inside.

The man seems familiar to her. He looks back toward the camera and winks at her. It's one of those winks that says "I'm taking care of it."

He says something she can't hear because there's no micro-phone—she could have gotten a model that had one, but she didn't think she'd need it. Still, she could swear that she can hear what the man is saying.

I love you, Sharon. I'll be right here with you.

Her hands start to shake and she tightens her grip on the phone. She brings it closer to her face in case the man says something else. He doesn't have a uniform on, now that she really looks. No FedEx or UPS or anything like that. He's wearing a tunic and bright orange Tevas. He wears a ball cap and toggles it up and down.

"Say it again," she whispers to the phone. Her heart hammers in her chest. "Please," she whispers. She thinks she recognizes Him after all.

Then the man looks full into the camera, His soft brown eyes seeing her, she's sure of it, and says, "I love you, Sharon. I love you, Sharon. I love you Sharon. I'll be right here with you."

And He just keeps saying it. He'll say it as many times as she needs to hear it.

11

— · —

Jesus Goes to the County Fair

You wouldn't believe the amount of prayer He hears coming from the fairgrounds. Mostly innocuous: *Lord, please let my pie win first place. God, help me get the ring around the fishbowl for once. Please, Jesus, just make the Tilt-A-Whirl stop—just make it stop.*

He's at this fair to talk to Bob, but that's not for a while yet. It will be darker than it is now when Bob realizes that he needs Jesus. In the meantime, Jesus strolls through the tents. He studies the woodworking exhibits, inhaling the sweet smell of sawdust. He admires the handcrafted birdhouses and stops to watch old men whittle whimsical figures out of gnarled hunks of wood. He appreciates the prize-winning pies, the rows of fig and fruit jellies, and a pumpkin so big maybe Cinderella really did ride in one to the ball. He gets confused looks—people wondering if He's part of an exhibit or a play that might happen later. Maybe after the clog dancing.

It's mostly the children who know it's really Him. They stop and tug on His tunic, hold their arms up to Him. Their parents think He's one of the performers who walk around the fair like that guy in the dragon costume. They click pictures with their phones.

"Smile with Jesus," some say, winking at Him—having "figured out" who He's supposed to be.

Back on the midway, Jesus pauses by one of the food stands. The food vendors are His favorite. He loved a fresh hunk of bread and some dried figs as much as the next guy back in His day, but this fair has funnel cake. The sweet deliciousness of the hot dough and powdered sugar is a delight.

He walks the crowded midway stopping to speak with folks here and there. The sky darkens and the lights pop on. Everything gets louder and livelier. A colorful chaos.

When it's time, He takes a seat on a bench beside the fortune teller's tent. Bob is just now looking into the crystal ball as Madam Midnight passes her hands over the empty orb and tells him with stoic sincerity that his future is unclear. Bob will then come out of the tent, still without the answers he so desperately wants and decide to buy a funnel cake. Jesus is a bit of a seer Himself.

As predicted, Bob comes out of the tent and heads for the light at the funnel cake cart. Jesus gets in line behind him. Bob looks back and does a double take.

He puts his hand to his thudding heart. "I thought you were Him for a second there."

"I am," Jesus says and winks.

Bob shakes his head and thinks *If only*. "Haven't I seen you before?" Bob asks.

"You have," Jesus says.

Bob looks more carefully at Jesus then. He wants to believe it could be true. Maybe this guy could be ...

"Did you find what you were looking for?" Jesus thumbs toward Madam Midnight and changes the subject, sort of.

"No," Bob says and sighs heavily. "I'm on a pretty scary ride. Scarier than any of these here, you know?"

"I do know," Jesus says. He knows what Bob means and He also remembers praying for His own "Tilt-A-Whirl" to stop, too. He could have just stopped it, but that didn't seem fair to the other riders. The "fully God" thing was cool, but the "fully man" thing sometimes left Him sick to His stomach.

The line moves forward and Jesus puts his hand on Bob's arm. "Did you know there was a pie tasting in the show tents up front?"

"They're closed by now," Bob says.

"I bet they're still open," Jesus says. "In fact, I'm sure of it."

Bob looks back toward the fortune teller's tent. "There wasn't anything in the crystal ball," Bob says. "It was just a piece of glass." Bob looks, then, into the deep brown of Jesus's gaze. "Maybe I will come with you. I like pie."

"Strawberry rhubarb," Jesus says and winks. "Heavy on the strawberry, light on the barb."

"Yes," Bob says, surprised.

"With a dollop of Cool Whip," Jesus adds. "I know."

Bob looks at Jesus. "Pie won't fix this, will it?"

"Not this time," Jesus says, his heart aching for Bob. Jesus puts his hand on Bob's arm. "I'll share a slice with you and at the end of the month there's an antique car show here. What say we meet then and talk about things?

Bob has some time yet, but it's not going to be easy. Jesus hates this part every time. He really does. Even though He knows they'll all meet up again, it hurts to watch them suffer. That's why He's at the fair—to make sure Bob isn't alone. Bob spends most of his time alone. Except when he's with his grandson. Jesus gets goosebumps again just thinking about that kid. Bob thinks his life hasn't mattered much but he's one in a long line of people who have led to that little boy who will one day do something amazing. It's the bigger picture. He'll tell Bob all about it.

Jesus puts his arm around Bob's shoulder and they start walking toward the pie.

"Sounds good," Bob says, some of the worry lifted from his voice. "Where will you be until then?"

"Oh, here, there, and everywhere," Jesus says. "I'm easy to find."

Bob nods his head and stands up a bit straighter. He puts his arm around Jesus's shoulder in return. Jesus leads Bob through the noise of the midway, past the dizzying lights of the Tilt-A-Whirl and into the soft and sweet quiet of his company.

12

— · —

Jesus Drives a '65 Mustang

Of course nobody would blame Jesus if He bought a set of vintage wheels and got out of Dodge. Arthur says as much to his daughter, Sharon, as they stand in the hallway just outside his son's hospital room while the nurses and aides do whatever it is they do after someone has died.

Sharon is quiet. She does that when she's trying to keep herself from dissolving into nothingness. Arthur tries to fill the silence by picking up a conversation they'd been having earlier before the pea fight in the cafeteria, but Sharon's breathing is getting choppy and so Arthur keeps his thoughts about the driving preferences of the Lord Most High to himself. Arthur is dealing with the death of his son, but he's also got to take care of his daughter, too. It's just what a father does.

Arthur holds Sharon's hand. While they wait Arthur imagines Jesus in a '65 red convertible Mustang. He's driving with the top down. He's got His arm resting on the window rim, His dark hair blowing around in the rushing wind, His olive skin soaking up the sun. He's headed to Starbucks to get a vanilla latte.

Jesus likes Arthur's daydream. Maybe Jesus will pull in at Starbucks and order that latte. Vente. Maybe an extra pump of something. Why not? He hears people talking to Him about the place all the time. *Jesus, Starbucks coffee is expensive.*

He laughs at His own joke.

Inside, His coffee costs the better part of a ten which He manifests out of His pocket. He gets a kick out of seeing "Jesus" written in Sharpie on the side of the cup—quotation marks and all. Outside, there are no tables empty, so Jesus has to beg a spot at someone else's.

"Story of my life," He says with a smile and sits down with a longhaired hippie.

The hippie tells Jesus he's trying to build a chicken coop.

"I can help with that," Jesus says.

He can almost feel the weight of the hammer in His hand and the metallic ting of the nails held tight in His teeth while He works.

"So you in, dude?" the hippie asks.

Jesus nods and tosses His empty cup into the trash. As He and the hippie walk through the parking lot, Jesus glances at the Mustang. He was on His way somewhere, wasn't He? He just meant to stop off for a caffeine buzz and then get back on the road.

But what's the point? No one even knows He's here. His sadness catches him off guard.

At the hippie's house, someone hands Jesus a hammer. It's a bit lighter than He thought it would be—a fiberglass handle perhaps. He's impressed with the evolution of tools. There's a pile of lumber scraps that Jesus figures is meant to be the coop. He pulls a couple of large beams loose and grabs some nails. He means to make a chicken coop—really He does. But He fashions a cross instead. He can't help himself. He rests it on His shoulder and turns back toward the highway. He remembers where He was going.

"Dude," the hippie calls out to Him.

Jesus raises one hand in a wave without looking back. He makes it through traffic to the Mustang and ties the cross to the top of the car. At least the trip will be easier on His back this time. Jesus pulls slowly into traffic, taking care with the cross. People honk and give Him the finger. He doesn't take it personally. They've got free will after all.

While He's driving, Jesus thinks about Arthur and Sharon and Andy in the ICU on the fourth floor. Time and place are circular so it's not like He really left. He's here in this car, sitting at a table in the hospital cafeteria, buying new shoes at the local shoe store, walking the city streets, serving those in need some tacos from a food truck, auditioning for a play, taking a comedy class, planning a wedding, sitting on a bench by the lake, picking up packages, eating a funnel cake at the fair, and sitting by Andy's bedside while Arthur and Sharon say goodbye to him—for now.

He wants to tell Arthur to go ahead and pray as much as he wants to; it never gets on Jesus's nerves, even when He's in the cafeteria. He doesn't like banana pudding anyway.

Jesus ignores the no parking signs and leaves the Mustang by the door. He goes up to the fourth floor and waits with Arthur and Sharon.

Later, outside the hospital, after Sharon and Arthur have said their goodbyes for the moment and Sharon has driven away, Jesus steps up beside Arthur and points at the car.

"Nice ride, huh?" Jesus says.

Arthur looks at Him and then looks again at the '65 Mustang, his mouth dropping open.

"Hop in," Jesus says now that this part is over and before the rest of it begins. "Let's tool around town for a while? If you don't mind my company."

"I could use it," Arthur says and they get into the car and drive away. "Was it worth it?" Arthur asks once they're out on the highway and headed into everything that comes next.

Jesus looks over at Arthur and smiles.

Arthur nods and says, "Yeah, it was for me, too. Even though it didn't turn out like I wanted it to."

Life hurts sometimes, but it's all worth it. And just like Arthur, Jesus knows that if He had to do it all over again, He still would.

13

— • —

Jesus Ignores Visiting Hours

Under the circumstances it's ok, really. And anyway, a fair amount of the time no one is paying attention to Him, but when they are, they let Him do what He wants. He just seems like He should be there, like the people who come around to deliver meals or drop off fresh linens. So even though visiting hours are over, Jesus waves the heavy ICU doors open and strolls past the nurses' station toward Andy's room. He slips inside and sits down beside Andy's bed. Andy's father and sister are down in the cafeteria talking about what sort of car Jesus would drive. He's heard many conversations about Himself, but that's a new one. New doesn't happen often and it makes Him smile. A red convertible. Flashy. Between that and His new bright orange shoes, He should really make a splash out in the world.

Jesus settles into the uncomfortable chair, ready to stay as long as Andy would like Him to.

Hello, Andy, Jesus says in the quiet of His heart.

Nothing registers on the cardiograph and all the monitors beep about as steadily as they ever did, but Andy hears Him.

Hello, Jesus.

They sit for a while, not saying anything, not needing to. This isn't the first time Jesus has been to visit Andy. They're old friends. But

Andy has a question he's been wanting to ask and he figures it's now or never.

Of course, Jesus answers him. *Of course you will.*

Andy is relieved. He needn't have worried.

I didn't always do the right things, Andy says. *I was mad sometimes about the way my life went.*

Jesus understood.

I'm not mad anymore, Andy says. *I hope I did a few things right along the way.*

You've done more good than you know, Jesus says.

Jesus knows that when He and Andy get back home that Andy will see how it has all come together for good. Sometimes Jesus wishes that people could see what He sees—how everyone is connected together like there are thin golden strands reaching from one person to the next—beautiful gossamer threads wrapped around wrists and twined into hair, floating from the windows, stretching across the seas. It's so beautiful it makes Jesus want to cry. If only they knew how much they all meant to each other, how much they were made for each other. Everything would matter so much more and so much less, depending.

Just wait, Jesus says to Andy, so excited for him to see. *It's so beautiful.*

When do we go? Andy asks.

Let's wait for your dad and your sister to come back, Jesus says. *They're downstairs starting a food fight.*

Andy laughs. The monitors beep and bleep and a nurse, Alison, pokes her head in. She startles when she sees Jesus sitting in the chair beside the bed. She freezes mid-movement so that her hand is outstretched toward the monitor she was about to check. She's so still that she stops breathing for just a moment.

Jesus sees the shimmer at her wrist and follows the golden thread to Andy's. The whole room is glittering with connections shooting out from Andy and Alison–out into the hallway, down to the cafeteria, out the front doors and across town to the theater, the comedy club, the shoe store, the taco food truck, the fair, and everywhere everywhere everywhere.

Jesus can feel every single thread. His skin tingles.

The nurse takes in a breath finally and steps closer to Andy's bed. She talks to Andy like he can hear her and Jesus appreciates that.

"Looking good, Andy," she says. "Hanging in there. I'll be back tomorrow afternoon to check in on you."

She stops at the door and looks back at Jesus. She's sure she's seen him somewhere before. She wants to say something, but can't get the words out. Jesus nods at her. *I know,* He says. She takes in a sharp breath and her eyes well with tears. She smiles and laughs and cries all at once as she heads back into the hall.

I'll miss her, Andy says, knowing he'll be gone by the time she comes in tomorrow.

You'll see her again, Jesus says. He tilts his head toward the door. *Here they come. They got peas everywhere.*

I'm ready, Andy says. *Let's say goodbye and blow this popsicle stand.*

Andy doesn't mean to make light of it. He knows that his dad and sister will be devastated, but he can already start to see the way things will play out. He's not sure how he sees it, but he does. They'll be ok. They will. And he'll see them again.

Andy's father and sister come into the room. Jesus is there, but they don't see Him. He lets them have their moments with Andy. This part is always so hard ... *ah, but wait ... just wait.*

After a while, when everyone is as ready as they're going to get, Andy and Jesus stroll back through the hall, past Alison at the nurses' station, and out the ICU doors into the main floors of the hospital.

Why is it so shiny in here? Andy asks. *Did they decorate?*

Jesus loves this part. He leads Andy along the yellow arrows on the floor that will point them toward the front door.

Whoa, Andy says when they step outside into a light he never knew how to imagine. Gold threads everywhere. The whole world is shimmering. *It's all so beautiful. Who did this?*

You did, Jesus says. *These are yours.*

Does everyone have them?

Yes, Jesus says. *They do.*

It all meant something, Andy says in awe.

Jesus puts his arm around Andy's shoulders. Indeed it does all mean something. All of it.

Let's get home, Jesus says. *You ain't seen nothing yet.*

Acknowledgements

Thank you to the many attendees of Wildacres Writers Workshop who have listened to me read these "Jesus stories" and encouraged me to continue writing them. Special thanks to Debra Daniel, who further encouraged me to put them all together in a collection and enter them into a writing contest. I didn't win that contest, but were it not for her insistence to enter, this book would still be a random collection of somewhat completed stories residing only in the recesses of my computer—and my heart. Thank you to Bill Spencer and Carolyn Elkins, who are my fairy godparents in all things. (Not that they're old enough to be, but that they're magic enough to be.) Thank you, as always, to my family, who love and support me in all things. And of course, all the thanks and glory to God the creator of all.

Thank you to the following journals in which a couple of these stories were originally published.

"Jesus Buys a Pair of Tevas" appeared in the 2015 issue of *Bacopa Literary Review.*

"Jesus Drives a '65 Mustang" appeared in *Solum Journal IV* in 2023.

About the Author

Amy Willoughby-Burle is an award -winning fiction author living in Asheville, NC with her husband and five children. When not working on her own fiction, she teaches high school literature and creative writing. She is also the director of Wildacres Writers Workshop. Her fiction focuses on the importance of faith, family, and friends and centers on the themes of forgiveness, second chances, and finding the beauty in the world around us. She is the author of the novels *The Lemonade Year*, *The Year of Thorns and Honey*, *The Other Side of Certain* and *Even if Nothing Else Is Certain*. Her short fiction has been published in numerous journals and in her collection *Out Across the Nowhere*. Visit her online at www.amywilloughbyburle.com.

—·—

HELP US SHARE HIS STORY

This little book is Adamant Amen Press's first title and a passion project. What's that passion? Letting people know how much Jesus loves them. Our little press doesn't have the means to promote far and wide (yet), so we're hoping that you'll take a moment to review this collection online wherever you like to leave reviews, to share it with your family and friends, or to spread the word about it to your groups and organizations. We'd love to put any money this collection makes back into the press so that we can publish more titles aimed at glorifying God through great fiction and telling people over and over how much Jesus love them. We would appreciate your help greatly.

Thank you,

Amy Willoughby-Burle/ Adamant Amen Press